A MAX LUCADO

CHILDREN'S TREASURY

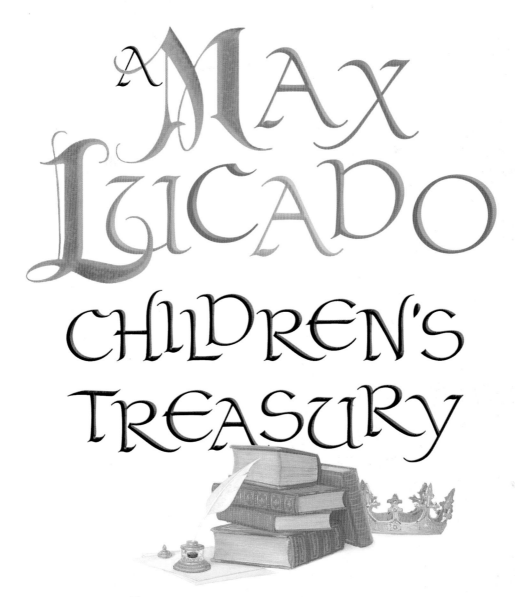

A Child's First Collection

THOMAS NELSON
Since 1798

NASHVILLE   DALLAS   MEXICO CITY   RIO DE JANEIRO   BEIJING

A Max Lucado Children's Treasury: A Child's First Collection

Just In Case You Ever Wonder
Text Copyright © 1992 by Max Lucado
Illustrations Copyright © 1992 by Toni Goffe
Library of Congress Control Number: 92-25059

The Crippled Lamb
Text Copyright © 1994 by Max Lucado
Illustrations Copyright © 1994 by Liz Bonham
Library of Congress Control Number: 94-19865

The Way Home
Text Copyright © 2005 Max Lucado
Illustrations Copyright © 2005 by Tristen Elwell
Library of Congress Control Number: 2005014506

Jacob's Gift
Text Copyright © 1998 by Max Lucado
Illustrations Copyright © 1998 by Robert Hunt
Library of Congress Control Number: 98-6490

Published in Nashville, TN, by Thomas Nelson. Thomas Nelson is a trademark of Thomas Nelson, Inc.

Thomas Nelson, Inc. titles may be purchased in bulk for educational, business, fundraising, or sales promotional use. For information, please email SpecialMarkets@ThomasNelson.com.

ISBN 10: 1-4003-1048-2
ISBN 13: 978-1-4003-1048-7

Printed in China
07 08 09 10 11 MULTI 9 8 7 6 5 4 3 2 1

Jenna, Andrea, and Sara, this book
is for you—just in case you ever wonder.

MAX LUCADO

Just In Case You Ever WONDER

Illustrated by Toni Goffe

THOMAS NELSON
Since 1798

NASHVILLE   DALLAS   MEXICO CITY   RIO DE JANEIRO   BEIJING

Long, long ago God made a decision—

a very important decision . . .

one that I'm really glad He made.

He made the decision to make you.

The same hands that made the stars *made you.*

The same hands that made the canyons *made you.*

The same hands that made the trees and the

moon and the sun *made you.*

That's why you are so special. God made you.

He made you in a very special way.

He made your eyes so they would twinkle.

He made your mouth so you could smile.

He made your laugh so you could giggle.

God made you like no one else.

If you looked all over the world—in every city in every house—there would be no one else like you . . .

no one with your eyes,

no one with your mouth,

no one with your laugh.

You are very, very special.

And since you are so special, God wanted to put you in just the right home . . .

    where you would be warm when it's cold,

    where you'd be safe when you're afraid,

    where you'd have fun and learn about heaven.

So, after lots of looking for just the right family, God sent you to me. And I'm so glad He did.

I'll never forget the first time I saw you . . .

  your eyes were closed,

  your fingers were curled in two little fists,

  your cheeks were puffy and round.

I knew in my heart God had sent someone very wonderful

for me to take care of.

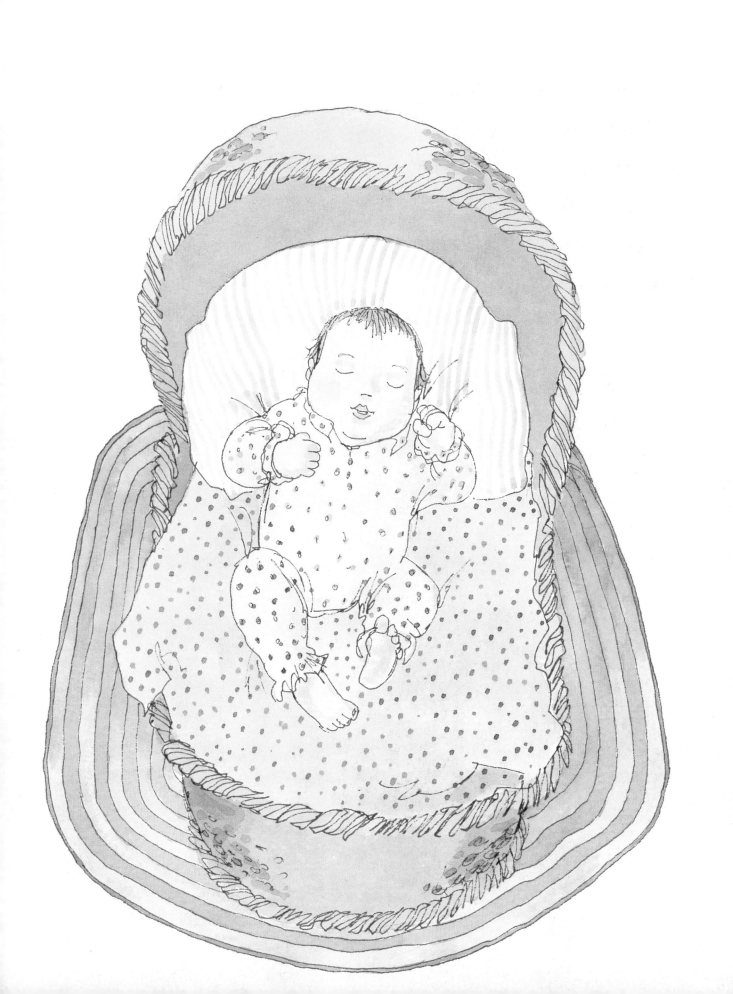

Your first night with me I heard every sound you made:

 I heard you gurgle,

 I heard you sniff,

 I heard your little lips smack.

 I heard you cry when you wanted to eat, and I fed you.

You're bigger now and do more things.

You can walk and run.

You can play and talk.

You can eat and sing and look at books.

You're not a little baby anymore.

But as you grow and change, some things will
stay the same.

I'll always love you.

I'll always hug you.

I'll always be on your side.

And I want you to know that . . . just in case

you ever wonder.

Remember I'm here for you.
On dark nights when you hear noises in your closet,
call me.

When you see monsters in the shadows, call me.

On hard days when kids are mean and don't treat you like they should, come to me.

If your grades are bad and your teacher is mad, come to me . . . 'cause I love you.

And I always will, just in case you ever wonder.

Most of all, I'll be here to teach you about God.

He loves you.

He protects you.

He and His angels are always watching over you.

And God wants me to make sure you know about heaven.

It's a wonderful place.

There are no tears there.

No monsters.

No mean people.

You never have to say "good-bye,"
   or "good night,"
   or "I'm hungry."
You never get cold or sick or afraid.

In heaven you are so close to God that He will
hug you, just like I hug you. It's going to be
wonderful. I will be there, too. I promise.
We will be there together, forever.
Remember that . . .
    just in case you ever wonder.

THE CRIPPLED LAMB

To our special friends—
Kelly, Kasey, and Kara Wilson

THE CRIPPLED LAMB

by Max Lucado
with Jenna, Andrea, & Sara Lucado

illustrated by Liz Bonham

THOMAS NELSON
Since 1798

NASHVILLE DALLAS MEXICO CITY RIO DE JANEIRO BEIJING

Once upon a time in a sunny valley, there lived a little lamb named Joshua. He was white with black spots, black feet, and . . . sad eyes.

Josh felt sad when he saw the other lambs with snow-white wool and no spots. He felt sad when he saw the other sheep with their moms and dads because he didn't have a mom or dad.

But he felt saddest when he saw the other lambs running and jumping, because he couldn't.

Josh had been born with one leg that didn't work right. He was crippled. He always limped when he walked.

That's why he always watched while the other lambs ran and played.
Josh felt sad and alone—except when Abigail was around.

Abigail was Josh's best friend. She didn't look like a friend for a lamb.
She was an old cow.

She was brown with white blotches that looked like rain puddles on
a path. Her belly was as round as a barrel, and her voice was always kind
and friendly.

Some of Josh's favorite hours were spent with Abigail.

They loved to pretend they were on adventures in distant lands. Josh liked to listen to Abigail tell stories about the stars.

They would spend hours on the hill, looking into the valley. They were good friends. But even with a friend like Abigail, Josh still got sad.

It made him sad to be the only lamb who could not run and jump and play in the grass.

That's when Abigail would turn to him and say, "Don't be sad, little Joshua. God has a special place for those who feel left out."

Josh wanted to believe her. But it was hard. Some days he just felt alone. He really felt alone the day the shepherds decided to take the lambs to the next valley where there was more grass. The sheep had been in this valley so long, the ground was nearly bare.

All the sheep were excited when the shepherd told them they were going to a new meadow.

As they prepared to leave, Josh hobbled over and took his place on the edge of the group.

But the others started laughing at him.

"You're too slow to go all the way to the next valley."

"Go back, Slowpoke. We'll never get there if we have to wait on you!"

"Go back, Joshua."

That's when Josh looked up and saw the shepherd standing in front of him. "They are right, my little Joshua. You better go back. This trip is too long for you. Go and spend the night in the stable."

Josh looked at the man for a long time. Then he turned slowly and began limping away.

When Josh got to the top of the hill, he looked down and saw all the other sheep headed toward the green grass. Never before had he felt so left out. A big tear slipped out of his eye, rolled down his nose, and fell on a rock.

Just then he heard Abigail behind him. And Abigail said what she always said when Josh felt sad. "Don't be sad, little Joshua. God has a special place for those who feel left out."

Slowly the two friends turned and walked to the stable together.

By the time they got to the little barn, the sun was setting like a big orange ball. Josh and Abigail went inside and began to eat some hay out of the feed box.

They were very hungry, and the hay tasted good.

For a little while, Joshua forgot that he had been left behind.

"Go to sleep, little friend," Abigail said after they finished eating. "You've had a hard day."

Josh was tired. So he lay down in the corner on some straw and closed his eyes. He felt Abigail lie down beside him, and he was glad to have Abigail as a friend.

Soon Josh was asleep. At first, he slept soundly,
curled up against Abigail's back. In his sleep he dreamed.
He dreamed of running and jumping just like the other sheep.
He dreamed of long walks with Abigail through the valley.
He dreamed of being in a place where he never felt left out.
Suddenly strange noises woke him up.

"Abigail," he whispered, "wake up. I'm scared."

Abigail lifted her big head and looked around.

The stable was dark except for a small lamp hanging on the wall. "Somebody is in here," Josh whispered.

They looked across the dimly lighted stable. There, lying on some fresh hay in the feed box, was a baby. A young woman was resting on a big pile of hay beside the feed box.

Joshua looked at Abigail, thinking his friend could tell him what was going on. But Abigail was just as surprised as Josh.

Josh looked again at the woman and the child, then limped across the stable. He stopped next to the mother and looked into the baby's face. The baby was crying. He was cold. The woman picked up the baby and put him on the hay next to her.

Josh looked around the stable for something to keep the baby warm. Usually there were blankets. But not tonight. The shepherds had taken them on their trip across the valley.

Then Josh remembered his own soft, warm wool.
Timidly, he walked over and curled up close to the baby.
"Thank you, little lamb," the baby's mother said softly.
Soon the little child stopped crying and went back to sleep.
About that time, a man entered the stable carrying some rags.
"I'm sorry, Mary," he explained. "This is all the cover I could find."
"It's okay," she answered. "This little lamb has kept the new king warm."
A king? Joshua looked at the baby
and wondered who he might be.
"His name is Jesus." Mary spoke
as if she knew Josh's question.
"God's Son. He came from
heaven to teach us about God."

Just then there was another noise at the door. It was the shepherds—the ones who had left Joshua behind. Their eyes were big, and they were excited.

"We saw a bright light and heard the angels . . ." they began.

Then they saw Joshua next to the baby. "Joshua! Do you know who this baby is?"

"He does now." It was the young mother who was speaking. She looked at Joshua and smiled. "God has heard your prayers, little lamb. This little baby is the answer."

Joshua looked down at the baby. Somehow he knew this was a special child, and this was a special moment.

He also understood why he had been born with a crippled leg. Had he been like the other sheep, he would have been in the valley. But since he was different, he was in the stable, among the first to welcome Jesus into the world.

He turned and walked back to Abigail and took his place beside his friend. "You were right," he told her. "God does have a special place for me."

The Way home

For our Brazilian princesses—
Paulina and Victoria Downing

The Way Home
a Princess Story

MAX LUCADO
ILLUSTRATED BY TRISTAN ELWELL

THOMAS NELSON
Since 1798

NASHVILLE   DALLAS   MEXICO CITY   RIO DE JANEIRO   BEIJING

ong, long ago, in a kingdom more majestic than any other, there lived a beautiful, young princess, Anna. Anna had not always been a princess. When she was an infant, the king had found her, abandoned in the forest, and brought her to the castle to raise as his own.

Yet as Anna grew, so did her curiosity. She wondered about the world outside the kingdom. What had she missed? What lay beyond the green gardens of the castle? Anna sighed. She propped her elbow on the ledge, rested her chin in her hand, and stared out the castle window.

Flowers dotted the meadow. Children splashed in the creek. Beyond the meadow, the dark forest loomed. What a beautiful day outside! What a bad day to be inside!

"Ahem! Princess," a voice called, "your studies."

"Yes, Sir Henry." Anna glanced again toward the forest. "Is it true?"

The round man looked up, raising his eyebrows. "Excuse me?"

"About the Lowlanders. I hear that they never work and their days are all filled with fun."

The tutor lowered his book. "Forget them! They mean us harm."

"But *all* I do is work. I'm just not sure I was meant to be a princess."

Sir Henry crossed the room and rested his hands on Anna's shoulders. "I have watched you since the day you arrived, and I have been your teacher since you were small. I have seen you blossom with your father's guidance. Listen to me. The forest is no place for anyone, especially the daughter of royalty. Those trees know an evil that does not sleep."

"But—"

Sir Henry interrupted by placing a finger on her lips. "Your studies. There is much to learn."

Anna nodded, but stole one last glance into the valley, wondering about life away from the castle.

Deep within the forest, three Lowlanders plotted and rummaged through costumes.

Ima and Gunnah usually shared a costume.

"Let's be donkeys," Ima offered.

"Not again. That suit is hot, and you stink!" Gunnah smirked.

Getcha pulled on a hood. "The princess will feel sorry for a poor, old hag."

Passing as hags wouldn't be hard for them. With hunched shoulders and warty noses, they looked the part. They were tree-stump shaped, with faces as bumpy as cobblestones and ears as pointy as oak leaves.

Getcha was the tallest, but if he were to stand near the princess, he'd barely come up to her waist.

"You two dress as a farmer," ordered Getcha.

"I'm on top!" Ima shouted.

"You got top last time," Gunnah objected.

"Yeah, and look what happened. I was brilliant. We nabbed three castle-dwellers."

"Silence!" Getcha interrupted, holding a finger skyward. "We have one shot at the princess. Olbaid will be angry if we fail." The three lowered their heads.

"Olbaid," whispered Gunnah.

"Olbaid," echoed Ima.

After a quiet moment, they resumed plotting. Getcha instructed, "Tomorrow, when the teacher brings the girl to the creek, you two distract him, and I'll lure her into the trees." He hissed and smiled his one-toothed smile. "Olbaid will be proud."

Back at the castle, the king shook his head. "Why?!" he asked his daughter's teacher. "Why is she so curious about the Lowlanders?" He stroked his square jaw and stared at his old friend.

"Maybe she wonders what her life would have been like if she had not become a princess," Sir Henry explained. "She hears rumors of their easy life."

"Easy!? Dwelling in a dark forest? Dodging the wrath of Olbaid?"

"She is young, Your Majesty."

"Yes, but she is mine." The king shook his head. "I've tried to tell her so many times. She is meant to do important things."

"Perhaps she will listen to me, Your Majesty," Edward said, stepping forward.

The king smiled at the young man who spoke. Edward was the strongest of his knights. "Indeed she might listen to you, Edward. She certainly notices you."

Edward's face blushed, but he did not smile. "We must put an end to these thoughts of the Lowland. Olbaid sees your daughter as a prize to be won."

The king stiffened at the sound of his archenemy's name. "You're right. Talk to her. Tell her how they poison minds and . . ." He paused. "Remind her once more how much I love her."

Sir Henry led Edward through grand halls toward a large door. He heard feet pattering on the other side and shook his head knowing Anna was dashing toward her desk from the window. As they entered, she reopened her book.

Anna looked at Edward and smiled. Her beauty stole his breath: black satin hair, rosy cheeks, deep green eyes. It wasn't long ago that he had avoided her. During the time that he had trained to be a knight, she had excelled at being a brat. How was she so suddenly pretty?!

"Edward?" Sir Henry reminded.

"Oh yes," he answered, clearing his throat. "With your permission, m'lady?"

She nodded.

"Your fascination with the forest troubles us, Princess."

"Have you met them, Edward?" Her excited voice betrayed her curiosity.

"The Lowlanders mean you harm."

"But I've heard they have nothing but fun."

"You've heard wrong. Avoid these servants of Olbaid."

She shrugged, but the tone of Edward's next words urged her to heed his caution. "Your father loves you so much, Anna."

She smiled. "And I love him, Edward. I know to be careful."

The knight nodded with uncertainty and then dismissed himself. Still worried, he walked through the halls, fearing the worst. He was right to do so.

The next day, Sir Henry kept watch as the princess waded in the creek. The blue sky and bubbling waters lifted his spirits.

Suddenly a voice called, "Oh friend, help!"

The teacher turned to see a farmer ambling toward him. The wide-brimmed hat and chest-length beard covered Ima's face. Gunnah, hidden within the long coat, groaned beneath the weight. Barely able to see, he tripped, causing Ima to wobble even more.

The sight of the odd man might have roused Sir Henry's suspicions, but the man's clumsiness stirred his compassion. He hurried toward him, unaware of a disguised Lowlander approaching the princess.

"Is it true what I hear, young woman? That you desire to visit the forest?"

Anna, knee-deep in the water, looked up with a trusting smile. "You know the Lowlanders?"

"Indeed I do."

The princess glanced toward her teacher, helping the old man. "But . . . I can't."

"It will take only a moment," the woman enticed, beckoning with a crooked finger.

Anna looked toward the castle, then back to the entrancing, little figure.

By the time Sir Henry had righted the clumsy farmer, the old woman had convinced Anna to follow her into the forest. "For just a peek," Getcha assured in his highest voice.

Only a few steps into the trees, Anna regretted her decision. She couldn't keep up with the woman. "This may be easy for you, but I'm too—"

"Too what?" Getcha snapped in his normal voice, turning with such speed that his hood flew off. Anna tried to scream, but couldn't. "Too tall? Too pretty? Too good for the Lowlanders? You're one of us now!" he proclaimed.

The princess turned to run, but the forest had closed behind her.

"Your king can't save you!" Getcha cackled, rubbing his hands together.

Meanwhile, Sir Henry and the villagers searched, but no one had seen where Anna had entered the forest.

The princess was gone.

When the king heard, he wept quietly. "Who took her?" he asked Sir Henry.

"I don't know," the teacher responded sadly.

Suddenly, Edward entered, pulling the farmer by the sleeve, leading him before the king. Gunnah, within the cloak, tripped on Edward's foot, sending the two imps sprawling.

The Lowlanders scurried to their feet. Edward drew his sword. The king motioned him back.

"Where did you take Anna?" the king demanded.

Ima snickered. "Take her? She went by choice."

"Liars!" defied Edward.

"Any evidence of resistance? She *wanted* to leave," Gunnah added.

The king shook his head sadly.

He knew the Lowlander spoke the truth.

And he knew that no one, except a Lowlander, could navigate the forest.

Would he ever see Anna again? His attendants assumed he wouldn't want to. To be kidnapped is one matter, but to *run away*?

He spun from the window and surprised them, "I will go after her."

Their response was quick. "But the forest?"

"I will cut a path."

"It is thick!"

"I am strong."

Silence hung. Finally, one knight dared: "But, she . . . has chosen them."

The king replied, "She has been my daughter much longer than she has been with them."

And so the king prepared to leave. Vested in his strongest armor, bearing his sharpest sword, emboldened by the kingdom's bravest heart, he stood at the castle gates. Edward offered to accompany him, but the king declined. "This is *my* job."

"But you will need help."

"I'll be fine. You wait here and guard the castle."

Edward straightened. "That I will do. When you return—with Anna—you'll find me waiting."

Sir Henry apologized again for his part in losing the girl. "You aren't to blame," the king said softly, placing a hand on Sir Henry's shoulder. "This battle was destined to happen."

People lined the castle walls, watching the king stride toward the trees. Without hesitation, he entered the forest, and with one mighty slash of his sword, ancient boughs began to tumble. The image of Anna crawling her way through the brushwood tormented him. His arms and legs bled from the thorns. Her cuts would be worse.

As the fog thickened, Lowlanders mounted resistance. Imps snapped at his legs. Swinging from above, they clawed his shoulders. Lacking courage to face him, they hid in the brush and darted from holes. One flash of the king's blade and they'd scamper into hiding. They could not slow his progress or lessen his resolve.

The forest ended abruptly. The king stepped into a clearing,
his clothing and skin torn.

He found Anna, confused, in the center of the village. The forest
dwellers had abandoned their huts. The princess didn't run, nor
did she approach her father. She stood frozen with shame.

He sighed. Her clothing and skin were shredded, her hair matted
and caught with burrs. Her back was already beginning to stoop
like a Lowlander. When he touched her shoulder, she stiffened.

"Come back with me," he offered.

She said nothing.

"Why would you stay?"

She had no answer. Not for her father. Not even for herself.

"Come back to the castle with me," he offered.

"I'm one of them now," she mumbled.

"But you weren't made for this."

The king was silent. He knew what had to be done.

"Looking for me?" The sound of Olbaid's voice made the monarch cringe. "Your daughter is content here."

"No one is content in your presence."

Olbaid's eyes glowed. His bat-winged cape hung to the ground, exposing clawed feet.

"I have come for Anna."

"She is mine—one of many to come. They cannot resist. You can't keep them from the shadows," Olbaid growled.

"I'll give you something better," the king offered.

"What could be better than the daughter of the king?!" Olbaid laughed, then realized what the king meant. "You wouldn't!"

The king's silence was his answer.

"Give yourself?"

Anna turned toward her father. "No," she prayed softly.

Olbaid risked no delay. He opened his cape, releasing legions of Lowlanders that rushed to swarm the king.

Soon Olbaid stood over the king's lifeless body. "Behold your king, Anna. His love couldn't save you, nor himself."

Anna rushed to her father. Her tears dropped onto his face. "What have I done?"

Olbaid yanked her up. "You have sealed your people's doom." He cocked his head, releasing high-pitched laughter. The Lowlanders jumped, danced, and screamed at the feet of their leader.

Anna stood still. "What have I done?" she asked herself again. Kneeling, she took the king's hand and pressed it to her face.

Then, she felt his hand move.

She searched his face. For years, when retelling this story, she would describe this moment. His eyes opened and sparkled as if saying, "They may try, but they can't kill me."

She stood. Olbaid commanded, "Grab her!"

"Stop!" her father declared, jumping to his feet. "You have no power over me or mine."

The Lowlanders crept backward. Olbaid did too, muttering. He and his defeated followers ducked into the forest.

Just then, Ima and Gunnah appeared. "We escaped! Anna is ours—"

Ima stopped. Gunnah ran into him. They stared at the king, then at the empty village.

"Uh . . . looks like we came at a bad time," Ima whimpered, slowly backing away. The two turned and ran between the trees.

The king turned to Anna, smiled, and extended his hand in her direction.

She still didn't understand. "I can't go back. I don't know the way."

"But, Anna, that is why I came." For the first time, she saw the opening, a path leading to the castle. Now she understood.

Placing her hand in his and her trust in him, she made her choice.

"Stay with me," the father invited. "I'll show you the way home."

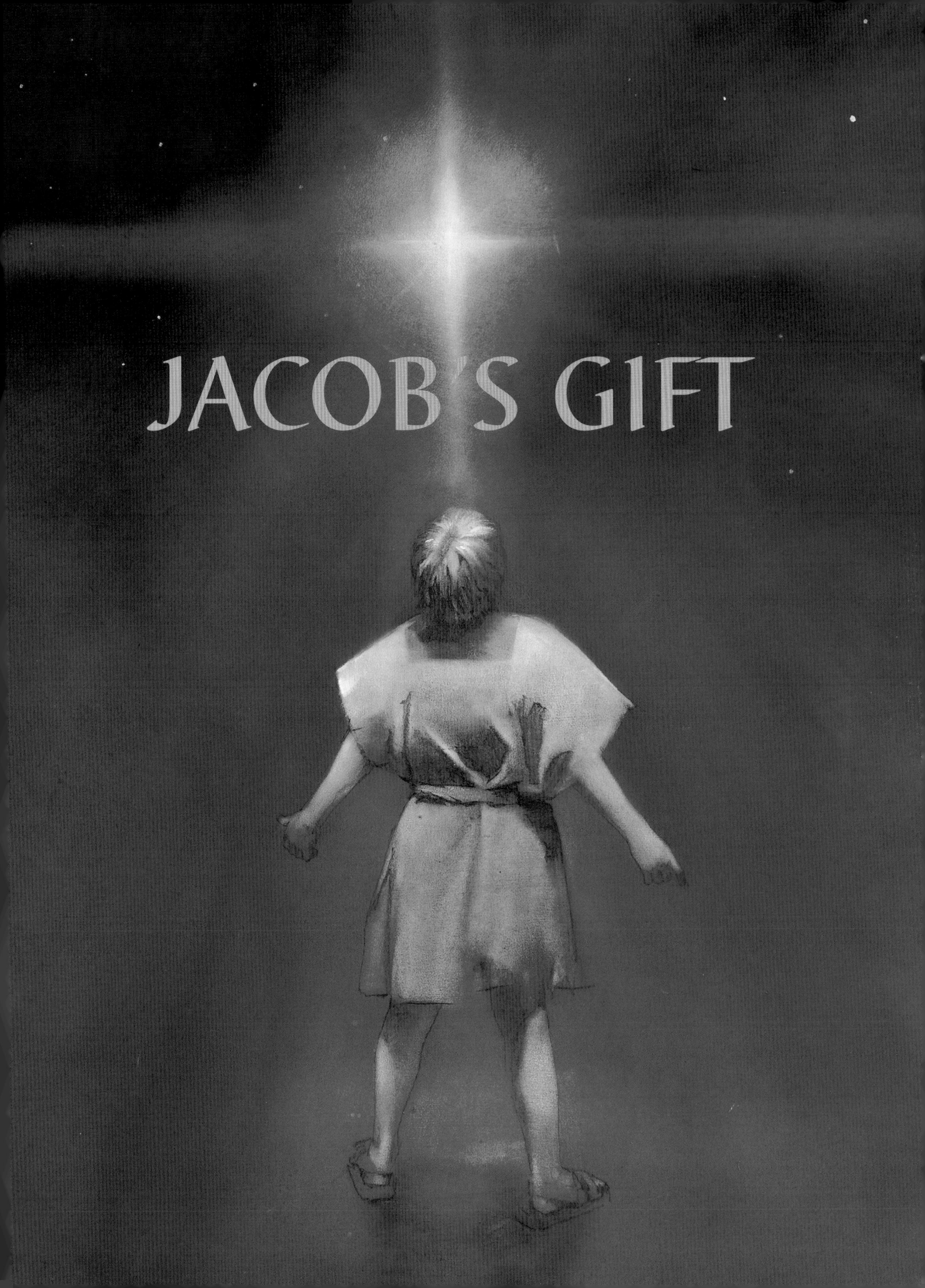
JACOB'S GIFT

For Allen and Maria Dutton,
your children and grandchildren—
Because you love Jesus.
Because you love Brazil.
And because you've loved us.

JACOB'S GIFT

Max Lucado

Illustrated by Robert Hunt

THOMAS NELSON
Since 1798

NASHVILLE   DALLAS   MEXICO CITY   RIO DE JANEIRO   BEIJING

Rabbi Simeon brushed the sawdust off his hands and began untying his apron. "Before you leave today, I have a special announcement." He hung the apron on a wooden peg and turned to look at the handful of boys in his shop. All but one apprentice had removed their aprons and put away their tools.

Rabbi Simeon looked across the workshop. One boy continued sawing a piece of wood.

"Jacob," the rabbi instructed, "our work is finished for the day. Put away your tools."

Jacob didn't respond. The only sound he heard was the *swish-swish* of the saw. And now, *swish-swish* was the only sound anyone heard. But Jacob didn't know that. The other boys in the shop began to snicker.

Rabbi Simeon let out a deep sigh and shook his head, but he wasn't mad. Deep down he was pleased. He, too, knew what it was like to get lost in the world of woodworking. But it was time to go home.

"Jacob!" the rabbi called again, his voice a little louder this time.

The sawing stopped. When Jacob heard no other noise, he knew he'd done it again. Slowly he placed his saw on the table.

"I'm sorry, Rabbi," he said softly.

Rabbi Simeon smiled. "It's all right. Put away your tools and hang up your apron."

Jacob quickly cleaned off his work area. With a sigh he stood and walked across the room, never looking up. This was the part he hated most. Everyone was looking at him. He hung up his apron as the other boys continued to snicker. Jacob's cheeks burned. Finally the rabbi spoke, and all eyes turned back to him.

"As I said earlier, my nephew from Nazareth should be here within a few days. He is a master carpenter who knows quality work. He will help me select one of you for a special task. The one who builds the best project will work with me on the new synagogue."

It will be me! The words were so strong in Jacob's thoughts, he feared he had spoken them out loud. Only days earlier he'd overheard the rabbi say, "Just leave Jacob alone with wood and he can do almost anything." Jacob had turned red then, too, but that time with pride.

I just have to be chosen, Jacob determined. *I want to use my hands to help build God's house. It doesn't matter if everyone says I'm so shy. This time . . .*

"Jacob, did you hear what I said?"

"Uh . . . no, sir."

"I'll be away for the next three days, but you may all use the workshop to finish your projects." As the others began to leave, the rabbi asked Jacob to stay.

Again, Jacob felt his cheeks warm. He waited until everyone had left and then approached the carpenter.

"I'm sorry, Rabbi," he apologized. "I'll do better next time."

The rabbi motioned for Jacob to sit on one of the stools. "Oh, Jacob, you've done nothing wrong. I asked you to stay so I could tell you something." The rabbi smiled, pulled up a stool, and sat down. He placed his big hand on Jacob's shoulder and began. "God has given you the gift of woodworking. What is difficult for many is easy for you. Surely, you've noticed."

Jacob nodded slowly. He had wondered why other boys struggled with the wood to make things that seemed so simple to him.

"God gives gifts, Jacob. Some can sing, others teach, and you—you can build. You have a special gift. Have you ever wondered why God gave you this gift?"

"So I can learn to be a good carpenter?" he guessed.

"Well," the rabbi chuckled, "not exactly. God gave you this gift to share with others. Let's say you gave a present to one of my daughters. How do you think that would make me feel?"

"Happy?"

"Of course. Even though you gave the gift to my child, I would feel like you had given it to me. God is like that, too. When we give a gift to one of His children, it's like giving a gift to God. If you ever have a chance to help somebody, remember what I told you.

"Now, run home and tell your father that I hope he has an inn full of guests next week."

That evening at supper Jacob's father reminded him of the days ahead. "We're expecting a lot of business, son."

"I'll get up early," promised Jacob. "I will work on my project in the mornings and help you in the evenings."

The next three mornings Jacob crawled out of bed while it was still dark and went to the workshop. With a fire going and a lamp burning, he worked hard to complete his project. The other boys laughed when he told them what he was going to build, but now that it was almost finished, they weren't laughing anymore.

Jacob was building a new kind of animal feed trough. His would have wheels. He got the idea while watching some men work in the stable next to his father's inn. They loaded a wagon full of hay, rolled it into the shed, and dumped it in the trough. He thought, *Why not put the wheels on the trough?* And that's what Jacob was planning to do.

Jacob had returned to the workshop after helping his father at the inn. *Rabbi Simeon will be here tomorrow; I must finish tonight*, thought the sleepy boy. Jacob looked at the trough and then at the four wheels piled on his workbench. *So much work still to do.* He was so tired. *Maybe if I close my eyes for a few minutes . . .*

In what seemed like the very next moment, a beam of starlight slipped through a crack and fell across Jacob's napping eyes. "What!" he shouted, startled by the sudden light. Had he slept through the night? Then he looked out and saw the village showered by a gleaming, shimmering light in the night.

Jacob rubbed the sleep from his eyes as he walked outside and toward the star that seemed to dance in the sky near his father's inn.

Then he heard a strange sound in the stable behind the inn. Quietly, Jacob crept closer. He looked through a knothole in the stable wall. There, in a tiny nest of straw on the ground, was a baby! Beside the baby knelt his mother. A man gently covered her with his cloak. *The baby must be uncomfortable on the ground,* Jacob thought.

Quickly, Jacob turned and raced back to the workshop. He stood beside his newly built feed trough. He had measured each board so carefully. He had cut each piece with skill. He had oiled it with care. It was the best work Jacob had ever done. Tomorrow the rabbi would select the best apprentice.

But tonight there's a new baby without a place to sleep. . . .

"Good morning, boys," said Rabbi Simeon. "This is the big day."

Jacob approached the rabbi. "Uh, sir . . . I need to tell you something."

"Later, Jacob. We need to get everything ready for my nephew. Here, help me." The rabbi's voice drifted off as he began to take the projects outside—an unfinished chair, a desk with one leg too short, and a wobbly stool. Then, looking at a stack of four wheels, he asked, "Where is your project, Jacob?"

"That's what I tried to tell you. Something happened. There was this big star and—"

"Uncle Simeon!"

"Joseph!" Simeon shouted, extending his arms. "I'm so glad you're here!"

Jacob's eyes widened. This was the man he had seen with the baby in the stable the night before. With one arm still around Joseph, the rabbi turned to Jacob.

"Jacob, this is my nephew from Nazareth."

Jacob was too surprised to speak, so Joseph spoke in his place. "We've already met," said Joseph, putting a hand on the boy's shoulder. "In fact, Jacob gave my newborn son his very first gift."

"Your son?" the rabbi inquired. "What son? Where is he?"

"Come, and I'll show you."

And the rabbi and Jacob hurried behind Joseph.

Joseph led them around a curve and down the hill toward the inn. "Did you stay at the inn, Joseph?"

"Not quite, it was too full." Joseph smiled.

"Then where did you stay?" asked Rabbi Simeon.

"You'll see." Joseph led them past the inn to the bottom of the hill. There he left the path and turned toward a shelter. "The stable?" Simeon asked. "You kept your baby in a—"

Joseph smiled and placed a finger to his lips. "Quiet, Uncle. They're asleep. Follow me." He lowered his head and entered the stable.

A cow mooed at the presence of the trio. Joseph stepped next to the trough and motioned for them to approach. When the rabbi and his student looked inside, they saw a beautiful newborn baby.

"His name is Jesus," Joseph whispered. "And he has a cradle fit for a king."

Joseph's kindness made Jacob's cheeks turn red. But he felt so good, seeing the baby asleep in the feed trough he had made.

"Now I see why your project was missing," said the rabbi, "and it's the finest project I've seen. You will be the one to help build God's house. But, tell me, why did you decide to give your feed trough away?"

Jacob smiled with delight.

"I remembered what you said, Rabbi. 'When you give a gift to one of God's children, you give a gift to God,'" said the boy.

The rabbi's voice was soft. "And so you have, my son. So you have."